■ ■ ■ ■ ■ ■ ■ ■ ■ ■

Junie B., First Grader
One-Man Band

BARBARA PARK

Junie B., First Grader
One-Man Band

illustrated by Denise Brunkus

SCHOLASTIC INC.
New York Toronto London Auckland Sydney
Mexico City New Delhi Hong Kong Buenos Aires

To the talented Denise Brunkus . . .
who draws Junie B. with a sense of style,
a sense of spirit, and—best of all—a sense of humor.
What a wonderful gift.

ISBN 0-439-63823-2

Text copyright © 2003 by Barbara Park.
Illustrations copyright © 2003 by Denise Brunkus. All rights reserved. Published by Scholastic Inc., 557 Broadway, New York, NY 10012, by arrangement with Random House Children's Books, a division of Random House, Inc. SCHOLASTIC and associated logos are trademarks and/or registered trademarks of Scholastic Inc.

12 11 10 9 8 7 6 5 4 3 2 1   5 6 7 8 9 10/0

Printed in the U.S.A.   40

First Scholastic paperback printing, March 2005

Contents

1

Kicking the Cow

Monday

Dear first-grade journal,

A KICKBALL ~~TORNAMINT!~~ TOURNAMENT

A KICKBALL ~~TORNAMINT!~~ TOURNAMENT

The whole entire first grade is going to have a KICKBALL ~~TORNAMINT!~~ TOURNAMENT!

My teacher told us that news last week. And I can't even stop thinking about it! Our ~~familys~~ families

are going to come and
everything!
   I have been practicing my
kicking every day after school.
   I can kick high and low. And
fast and slow. And to and fro.
And pro and con.
   When I grow up I will have
my own kicking show on TV,
probably.
                From,
                Junie B., First Grader

I smiled at that nice thought.
   Then I peeked over the side of my desk.
And I tried to wiggle my piggy toe.

It still felt sore.

That's because yesterday a little trouble happened when I was practicing in my backyard. And it's called, I accidentally kicked my ball over the fence. And I didn't want to go get it. So I had to find something else to kick.

And then ha!

I spied Mother's brand-new watering can!

It was the one with the funny cow painted on it.

And it was sitting right out in the middle of the yard!

I laughed out loud at that perfect target!

"I bet I can kick that silly cow right over the moon!" I said.

Then I rubbed my hands together very excited.

And I backed all the way up to the fence.

Then *VA-ROOM!*

I took off running!

And *ZOOM!*

I ran faster and faster!

And *KA-BOOM!*

I kicked that can as hard as I could!

And *OWIE OW OW!*

That dumb-bunny can was filled full of *water*! And nobody even told me about that problem!

I fell down in the grass very painful.

Then I rolled around and around. And I hollered real loud.

"MY TOE! MY TOE! MY TOE!" I hollered. "MY TOE! MY TOE! MY TOE!"

Mother hurried to the back door.

"Junie B.! Oh my goodness! What's wrong?" she called.

"MY TOE IS WRONG! MY TOE IS WRONG! 911! 911!" I yelled.

Mother hurried outside and took off my shoe and sock. She looked at my toe.

"OW OW OW!" I yelled again.

Mother hugged me. "What in the world did you *do* to hurt it so badly?" she asked.

"Did you trip over a rock or something?"

I did a gulp.

'Cause maybe I shouldn't mention that I kicked her can, possibly.

Mother waited for me to answer.

Then, very slow, her eyes glanced over to her cow.

He had a giant dent in his head.

Also, his nose did not look normal.

Mother did a frown. "Junie B.?" she said very suspicious. "What's the story here?"

I looked back at her real impressed.

That woman is sharp as a tack, I tell you.

Finally, I did a sigh. And I told her the story here.

"Yeah, only this wasn't even my fault, Mother," I said. "It really, really wasn't. On account of at first I was practicing my kicking. And then my ball went over the fence. And so what was I supposed to do? Kick air?"

I did a thumbs-up.

"But good news!" I said. "'Cause just then I saw your cow can! And so I ran at him with all my might! And then I kicked him as hard as I could!

"Only too bad for me. 'Cause that stupid thing was filled with water! And now I have a smashed piggy toe."

I thought for a minute.

Then I folded my hands in my lap very quiet.

"The end," I said.

Mother did not look happy with me. "Gee, imagine that. A *watering* can actually had *water* in it. How unusual," she said.

That is called sarcastic, I believe.

After that, Mother carried me inside. And she called the doctor. And he told her to raise it up on a pillow and use ice.

And so guess what?

At first, it felt a little better.

Only this morning when I got dressed, it hurt to put on my shoe. And so—even though it was chilly outside—Mother said I could wear sandals to school.

And so that's how come I keep checking on it this morning. To see if it's feeling any better.

I closed my journal real quiet. Then I bent over in my chair. And I patted my toe very gentle.

Next to me, May made a face.

"You shouldn't play with your feet, Junie Jones," she whispered. "Playing with feet is what stinky people do."

I stuck out my tongue at that girl.

I still get a kick out of that behavior.

After that, I sat back up again. And I stacked my first-grade dictionary on top of my journal.

Then I laid my head on my desk. And I daydreamed about the kickball tournament some more.

In my dream, I was the only person in Room One who could kick the ball.

That's because all of the other children in Room One had broken legs. On account of accidents happen sometimes.

And so I played in the tournament all by myself.

And I won the whole darned thing without any help!

I was the star of Room One!

All of my friends shouted and cheered.

Then they hugged me very happy. And they threw confetti on my head.

Only not May.

May threw a small potato.

That was uncalled for, I believe.

2

More Piggy Problems

I stayed in my daydream a real long time. Also, I think I snored a little bit.

Then—all of a sudden—*SMACK!*

Mr. Scary clapped his loud hands together!

And that noise scared the daylights out of me, I tell you!

I jumped straight up in my seat. And my arms flinged out very crazy!

Then my hand knocked into my dictionary!

And oh no! Oh no!

That heavy book went over the edge of my desk! And it landed on my sore toe!

"OW!" I shouted real loud. "OW OW OW OW OW!!"

I reached for my foot. And I started to cry.

Mr. Scary came running back to me.

Then he quick sent Herbert to the school nurse to get some ice.

And hurray for Herbert! 'Cause he brought that woman back with him!

Her name is Mrs. Weller.

I know her from previous accidents.

Mrs. Weller gave me some tissues. And she put an ice bag on my piggy toe.

It felt heavy and soggy on that sore guy.

I pulled my foot away. But she put it right back again.

"Please, Junie B.," said Mrs. Weller. "If

you just keep this ice on your toe, it will start to feel better. I promise."

I shook my head real fast.

"No, it won't, Mrs. Weller," I said. "I *know* it won't. 'Cause Mother already put ice on that same toe yesterday. But today it still hurt. And that's how come I had to wear sandals to school."

"Oh, dear," she said. "You mean this poor toe was already injured before you came to school today?"

I did a sniffle.

"Yes," I said. "It was injured a real lot, Mrs. Weller. On account of yesterday I kicked a cow. And that thing was solid as a rock, I tell you."

Mrs. Weller's face went funny.

"You . . . you kicked a *cow*?" she said real soft.

"Yes," I said. "And the cow was full of water. And a cow full of water doesn't even budge."

After that, Mrs. Weller got very speech-less. And she didn't ask any more questions. She just kept holding the ice bag on my foot. Plus also, she mumbled to herself.

Room One stretched their necks to see my foot.

Then Shirley stood up. And she said that she knows just how I feel. 'Cause one time she accidentally kicked a brick. And that did not feel good, either.

And then Roger said he hurt *his* toe before, too. 'Cause last year he accidentally kicked a refrigerator-repair truck.

Plus a boy named Sheldon said that last summer, he accidentally kicked a giant tree stump. On account of his cousin told him it was made out of rubber.

"Only it wasn't," said Sheldon very upset. "It was made out of *tree*. And so all of my toes got their heads bashed in."

After that, Sheldon put his foot up on his desk. And he started taking off his shoe to show us.

Mr. Scary held up his hand. "No, Sheldon. Please. That's *really* not necessary," he said.

But Sheldon quick yanked off his shoe and sock. And he raised his piggies way high in the air.

"See, everybody? See the baby one? The baby one still has a little red knob on the side of it," he said. "See?"

Just then, Sheldon tipped his chair back on two legs so he could raise his foot even higher.

Only too bad for him. Because, quick as a blink, his chair legs slided out from underneath him.

And *BOOM!*

He went crashing into the aisle! And his forehead got a knob on it! Just like his baby toe!

Mrs. Weller quick grabbed the ice bag from my foot. And she put it on Sheldon's head.

She said he needed to come to the office with her right away.

Only wait till you hear this!

Sheldon didn't even *cry*!

Instead, he left the ice bag on his head. And he put his shoe and sock back on very calm. And he walked to the door with Mrs. Weller.

All of us clapped and clapped for that brave boy.

Sheldon smiled when he heard that.

Then he turned around.

And he did a bow.
And the ice bag fell off his head.

3

More Bad News

Mother came to get me from school that day. She said she would drive me and Sheldon home so we wouldn't have to take the bus.

I walked to the parking lot very limping.

Sheldon was still wearing the ice bag on top of his head.

"My. It must have been *quite* a day in Room One," said Mother.

Sheldon did a sigh. "I've had better," he said.

After that, both of us got in the backseat. And we buckled our seat belts.

Sheldon quick put his window down.

Mother turned around. "Gee, I don't know, Sheldon," she said. "That's going to be a lot of wind on you, don't you think?"

"I like wind," said Sheldon. "Wind makes my cheeks flap."

Mother stared at him a second. "Okey-doke," she said kind of quiet.

Then she turned back around. And she started the car. And we drove out of the parking lot.

Sheldon leaned his head close to the window. And he tilted his head into the rushy air.

He opened his mouth so the wind flapped his cheeks.

Both of us started to laugh.

Only just then, a little bit of trouble

happened. 'Cause Mother went around a corner kind of whizzy.

And Sheldon's head got tilted even further.

And *WHOOSH!*

The ice bag blew right out the window!

Sheldon sat very still after that.

Finally, he closed the window. And he drummed his fingers on the seat.

"Today isn't really going that good for me," he said.

I nodded.

Then I patted his arm.

'Cause sometimes I understand that boy perfectly well.

That night, I tossed and turned in my bed. 'Cause my toe did not like things touching it, that's why. Not even the sheet.

Only here is the worstest part of all.

Because the next morning—when I took off my covers—MY WHOLE ENTIRE TOENAIL WAS BLACK!

I did a scream at that terrible sight!

Mother and Daddy came running.

"Junie B.! What on *earth* is the matter?" said Mother.

"MY TOE IS THE MATTER! MY TOE IS THE MATTER!" I hollered back. "LOOK! LOOK! LOOK!"

I held up my foot for Mother to see.

"Oh, my," she said. "The doctor said this might happen. Your toenail has a bad bruise on it."

I wrinkled my eyebrows at her.

"A *bruise*?" I said. "That's all it is? It's just a *bruise*?"

Mother nodded. "Yes. It's just a bruise,

Junie B.," she said. "But I'm afraid it's going to be a little painful to wear shoes for a while."

Daddy sat down next to me.

"Don't worry, though, honey," he said. "As soon as it grows out, it will look normal again."

He pointed to his bare foot. "Look at mine. I've bruised my big toenail many times over the years. But it's always grown out as good as new. See?"

I looked at it and made a face.

Daddy's big toe is not attractive.

Just then, tears came in my eyes.

I touched my toe very gentle.

"Ow! Ow! Ow! It hurts even worser than yesterday," I said. "And so now what am I supposed to do? 'Cause I don't even want to wear sandals to school again. On account of sandals don't protect toes from getting hurt."

Mother thought for a minute.

Then she went to my closet. And she got out my old red sneakers. And she cut a hole in the top of one of them with my scissors.

She held it up for me to see.

"Ta-daaaaa," she said real singy.

And ha! What do you know? The hole was right where my sore piggy toe would be!

Mother helped me put on my red socks. Then she slid the holey sneaker on my foot very careful.

And surprise, surprise!

It didn't even hurt, hardly!

After breakfast, Mother drove me to school again.

Only at first, when I went to my room, I

felt kind of shy about my sneaker hole. And so I snuck to my seat and I showed it to my friend Herb in private.

And guess what?

Herbert's whole face lighted up.

"A *window*," he said. "You've got a *window* in your shoe."

I did a giggle at that idea.

"Hey, yeah," I said. "A *piggy toe* window."

Just then, Sheldon came hurrying into Room One.

He had a shiny red Band-Aid on his forehead.

He stood in the front of the room. And he pointed to it with his finger.

"No one touch this, please!" he said real loud.

He turned to Mr. Scary.

"Even though I came back to school today, I'm still not totally right up here," he said.

Mr. Scary nodded. "Oh yes, Sheldon. I'm very aware of that," he said.

Sheldon kept on talking. "I probably shouldn't play in the kickball tournament on Friday, either," he said. "'Cause what if I'm standing at home plate . . . and a ball starts rolling at me . . . and then it hits a rock . . . and it bounces up and smacks me in the Band-Aid . . . and I get a bump on top of my bump?"

He did a little shiver. "Double bumps would not be good," he said.

Mr. Scary looked at him.

"No, Sheldon. Double bumps would *not* be good," he said. "But don't worry. Between now and then I'm sure we can come up with something else you can do in the tournament."

After that, Mr. Scary glanced over at me. "And don't *you* worry, either, Junie B.," he said. "We'll think of something else you can do, too. Okay?"

I raised my eyebrows at that guy.

"Yeah, but I don't want to do something else, Mr. Scary," I said. "I want to play in the kickball game. I've been practicing really hard."

Mr. Scary smiled kind of sad.

"Yes. I'm sure you have, Junie B.," he said. "But your toe is already sore. And I doubt if you'll feel like kicking a ball with it by Friday."

I sat there a minute.

'Cause I never even thought of that problem before.

All of a sudden, my shoulders felt very slumping.

I put my head on my desk. And I hid under my sweater.

'Cause now I would *never* be the star of the kickball tournament.

And that had been the happiest day-dream of my life.

4

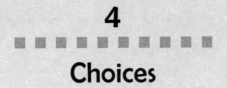

Choices

Tuesday

Dear first-grade journal,

  Recess was not fun today.

  I sat on the playground.

And I stared at my sore toe

through my piggy toe ~~winde~~ window.

  Sheldon sat next to me.

  He kept pressing on his red

Band-Aid and saying OUCH!

  I told him to ~~nock~~ knock it off.

I am not in a good ~~mooed.~~ mood,
        From,
        Junie B., First Grader

After I got done writing, I heard talking in the front of the room.

I looked up.

Lucille was standing at Mr. Scary's desk.

Camille and Chenille were standing there, too.

All of them were blabbering at the exact same time.

Mr. Scary covered his ears.

Finally, he said *whoa, whoa, whoa* at them. And he pointed for them to sit back down.

After that, Mr. Scary stood up. And he

walked to the front of the room.

"Boys and girls . . . it has come to my attention that not *everyone* in Room One wants to play in the kickball tournament," he said.

His eyes glanced over to Camille and Chenille.

"It seems that two of our classmates would rather be cheerleaders," he said. "And another one would like to be—"

This time, his eyes glanced at Lucille.

"—homecoming queen," he said.

Lucille sprang right up.

"No, no. *Princess!*" she called out. "I want to be homecoming *princess,* Mr. Scary! *Not* queen! Princesses are way cuter than queens. Plus princesses aren't old."

She looked at the children and fluffed herself.

"Wait till you see me, everyone. I'm going to have a beautiful float made out of pink rose petals," she said. "And there will be a golden throne for me to sit on."

She looked all around the room.

"Maybe a few of you girls might like to be my attendants," she said. "But my nanna will have to look you over first."

Mr. Scary went to the sink in the back of the room. And he took an aspirin.

Room One started buzzing about Lucille.

Then some of the children started thinking about different jobs that they could have in the tournament, too.

"Hey! Maybe I can be the game announcer on the loudspeaker," said Roger.

"And after the game I can pour root beer on all the winners!"

"Yeah," said Shirley. "And I could sell Rice Krispie Treats! My mother says those things are all profit."

Just then, May jumped up.

"And *I* could do crowd control!" she called out. "'Cause I already have a badge at home. And so all I'll need is a big stick to poke people with. And a gas mask."

Mr. Scary took another aspirin.

Then he walked back to his desk. And he took a deep breath.

"Okay. Here's the best I'm going to do for you guys," he said. "I'll give everyone in here two choices of jobs. You can either play in the game as part of the team. *Or* you can be a cheerleader. But that's it. That's my best offer."

Lucille stood up at her desk. She flounced her dress very upset. Then she plopped back down again.

After that, Sheldon stood up, too. And he pointed to his Band-Aid.

"But what about *this*, Mr. Scary? Have you forgotten about my injury?" he asked. "I *can't* play in the game, remember? And cheerleading is just for *girls*."

Mr. Scary frowned. "Well, that's not actually true, Sheldon. Lots of colleges have male cheerleaders," he said. "But since you and Junie B. *both* have injuries, I'll let you two pick different jobs to do in the tournament. Okay? That would only be fair."

Sheldon looked relieved.

"Yes!" he said. "I was hoping you'd say that! Because I already know what I'm going to do!"

He quick climbed on his chair and made a 'nouncement.

"I'm going to do a halftime show! I'm going to do a halftime show!" he shouted.

Mr. Scary grabbed him and put him back in his seat.

"A halftime show?" he asked, kind of curious.

Sheldon nodded real fast.

"Yes! Yes! Yes!" he said. "'Cause my dad used to play the cymbals in his high school band! And he already taught me how. Plus he still has his band uniform! So my mother can fix it to fit me! And then I can march and play the cymbals like a real professional band guy!"

Sheldon clapped his hands together.

"And wait! Here's another idea! Maybe I can sing, too! 'Cause I learned some songs at Christmastime. And my dad says I can almost carry a tune!"

Mr. Scary smiled.

"You know what, Sheldon? I think that's a *fine* idea," he said. "In fact, I think a little halftime entertainment would be *excellent*."

Sheldon clapped some more.

"Yay! I'll start practicing as soon as I get home!" he said.

Mr. Scary smiled again.

Then he raised his eyebrows. And he looked back at me.

"So . . . Junie B.? What do you think? If Sheldon does a halftime show, would you like to be in it, too?" he asked. "I bet playing an instrument wouldn't be too hard on your sore toe. And I'm sure Sheldon would be happy to have another band member."

I did a loud groan.

Then I put my head back on my desk.
And I covered up with my sweater
again.

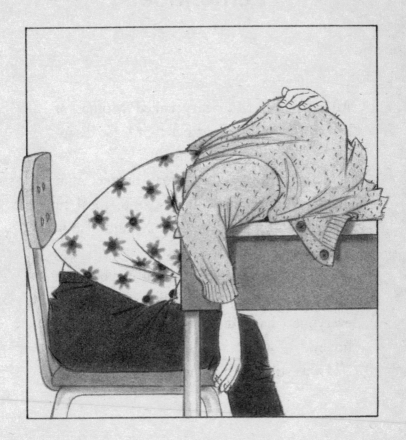

5

Lemonade

After school, Mr. Scary called Mother at her work. And he told her that I got disappointed about the tournament.

That's how come—for dinner that night—Mother made my favorite meal of pasketti and meatballs. Plus she and Daddy tried to be extra nice to me.

"I know you're upset about not being in the kickball game," Mother said. "But everyone has disappointments in life, honey."

I was still in a bad mood.

"I *hate* disappointments. I hate them," I said.

Daddy patted me. "Yes, well, we all hate being disappointed, Junie B.," he said. "But Mr. Scary said you can still do something fun in the tournament."

I did a mad breath. "I *hate* that dumb tournament. I hate it," I said.

Daddy squinted his eyes at me.

He said to please stop saying *hate*.

"I *hate* saying *hate*. I hate it," I said.

After that, Daddy picked me up. And he carried me to my room for a time-out.

It was not unexpected.

I waited till he was gone.

"I *hate* time-outs. I hate them," I whispered to my stuffed elephant named Philip Johnny Bob.

I hate them, too, Junie B., he said back.

*I hate everything you hate. You and me
hate everything exactly the same.*

I hugged him very tight.

I love that guy.

After that, both of us flopped on my
bed. And we calmed ourself down.

Pretty soon, Mother came and got me.
And she took me back to the table.

I did not talk to Daddy.

Also, I did not talk to my baby brother named Ollie. 'Cause he is just learning words. And all he keeps saying is *moo*.

Mother tried to be nice some more.

"Are you *sure* you wouldn't like to be a cheerleader, Junie B.?" she said. "I know you couldn't jump up and down on your sore toe. But you could still yell and shout for your team."

Daddy did a chuckle. "And yelling and shouting are right up your alley," he teased.

I did not laugh at that remark.

Daddy poked me. "Oh, don't be so glum," he said. "Being a cheerleader wouldn't be so bad, would it? *Every* little girl likes cheerleading."

I rolled my eyes at the ceiling.

"But I'm *not* every little girl, Daddy. I

am just *me*. Junie B. Jones. And I don't *want* to be a cheerleader. I want to be on the kickball team."

Just then, my nose started to sniffle very much.

"I even had a daydream about it," I said. "I was the star of the whole entire game. And it was very wonderful. Only now that is never going to happen."

Mother gave me a hug. "Well, no one can be a star *all* the time," she said. "It's just like I said earlier. Everyone has disappointments sometimes."

"Right," said Daddy. "And when life hands you lemons, you have to learn to make lemonade."

I looked weird at that man.

"Huh?" I said. "What's lemonade got to do with this?"

Mother smiled. "It's just a *saying,* Junie B.," she said. "It means that when life goes a little bit sour, you need to find a way to sweeten it up a bit."

Just then, Daddy went to the refrigerator. And he took out three lemons.

"Here, look. I'll show you," he said.

He held up the lemons for me to see.

"See what I have here?" he said. "They're just three sour old lemons, right?"

I did a shrug. "I guess so."

Daddy grinned. "Ahhh . . . but maybe these sour lemons are more fun than they look," he said.

Then, one by one, he threw each lemon into the air.

And WOWIE WOW WOW!

HE STARTED TO *JUGGLE* THEM!

I *mean* it!

He *did*!

My daddy juggled those lemons way high in the air! And I didn't even know that he *had* that talent!

I clapped and cheered very thrilled.

Ollie clapped, too.

Also, he said *moo*.

Then all of us started to laugh.

And Daddy did a bow.

"Do you see what I mean now?" he asked. "I turned three sour lemons into something more fun."

"And you can do the same thing, Junie B.," said Mother. "All you have to do is think of something fun to do in the kickball tournament. And then your sour situation will turn happy, too. Understand?"

I nodded very fast.

"I *do*, Mother! I do understand," I said.

"And guess what else? I think I already know what I'm going to do!"

I jumped down from my chair. And I picked up the lemons from the counter.

"I think I'm going to *juggle*!" I said very joyful. "I'll juggle in Sheldon's halftime show! And then everyone will clap and cheer! And I will be the star of that whole production!"

After that, I stood in the middle of the kitchen, just like Daddy did.

And one by one, I threw each lemon into the air.

I kept my eyes on them very perfect.

Only too bad for me. Because two of them crashed into the table. Plus the other one hit Ollie in the head.

He started to cry.

I patted him real fast.

Then I quick picked up the lemons. And I hurried up to my room.

'Cause juggling was going to take a little practice, apparently.

And there were only three days left until Friday!

6

■ ■ ■ ■ ■ ■ ■ ■ ■ ■ ■

Practicing

Wednesday

Dear first-grade journal,

Last night Daddy helped me

~~praktise~~ practice my juggling.

I kept on throwing those lemons into the air. And they kept on crashing into my floor.

Finally, I got ~~fusstration~~ frustration in me. And I threw them as high as I could.

The first one cracked my
ceiling light.
   The next one fell on my bed
and ~~rocked~~ knocked out my Raggedy
Andy named Larry.
   Lemons are not as easy as
they look.
   Friday is only two more days
away.
   I am getting stress in me.
         From,
         Junie B., First Grader

As soon as I finished writing, Mr. Scary
walked to the front of the room. And he
asked us to put away our journals.

   "Boys and girls, there are a few more

things I need to tell you about the kickball tournament on Friday," he said. "For
one thing—today and tomorrow—we'll
be taking extra-long recess periods to get
ready."

He looked around the class.

"Those of you playing on the team will be practicing on the softball field. And those of you who are cheerleaders will be practicing on the sidelines," he told us.

Camille and Chenille jumped right up from their seats.

"Mr. Scary! Mr. Scary! We have good news!" said Camille.

"Yes, we *do*!" said Chenille. "Our mother was a cheerleader in college. And last night she taught us some cheers!"

"Right!" said Camille. "And so today Chenille and I can teach them to the other girls!"

Mr. Scary smiled very pleased.

"That's *excellent* news, girls," he said. "I'll put you two in charge of teaching the cheers. Then I will have more time to work with the kickball team and the halftime show."

He looked back in my direction.

"Oh . . . and speaking of the halftime show, have you made a decision about what you want to do yet, Junie B.?"

I started to nod real happy.

Then, all of a sudden, I stopped.

On account of what if I told Room One that I was going to juggle in the halftime show? Only I still couldn't learn that talent by Friday?

Then some of the children might shout *BOO* at me. Plus others might laugh and laugh.

I tapped on my desk very thinking.

BUT—on the *other* hand—maybe I should just tell my class the whole entire truth. 'Cause Mother says the truth is *always* best. Only that is not the truth, of course. But maybe this one time, the truth might be the easiest.

"Junie B.?" said my teacher again.

I stood up at my desk. And I looked at Room One in their eyes.

"Okay . . . here is the whole entire truth," I said. "I am *trying* to learn how to juggle for Sheldon's halftime show. Only please do not get your hopes up, people. 'Cause I maybe might not learn it in time. And so—if I don't juggle at halftime—there is no laughing or booing allowed. And I *mean* it."

I quick sat back down again.

Lennie and Herb turned around in their seats.

"Whoa! You're learning to *juggle*?" said Lennie. "That's cool."

"Yeah, it *is* cool," said Herbert. "I wish I could juggle."

May rolled her eyes.

"*I* don't," she said. "What's so fun about throwing stuff in the air? And anyway, juggling is only for the circus. Who ever heard of juggling in a halftime show?"

I wrinkled my eyebrows very serious.

"Hmm . . . that's a good question, May. Let me think," I said.

Then I leaned real close to her face.

"ME! THAT'S WHO!" I said.

Lennie and Herb laughed very hard.

Then Sheldon looked back at me. And he gave me a happy thumbs-up.

I smiled.

'Cause what do you know?

This time, the truth worked beautifully.

7

Fun with Me and Sheldon

At recess, Mr. Scary got the kickball team started on their practice.

Then he came over to Sheldon and me. And he helped us with our halftime show.

First, he gave me a woodblock from the music teacher's room. Plus also, he gave me a drumstick.

"If you hit this woodblock while you march, you and Sheldon will be able to stay in step," he explained.

I smiled very thrilled. 'Cause hitting stuff is right up my alley.

I whacked that thing with my drum-stick.

Then Sheldon crashed his cymbals together.

And ha! That was beautiful music!

After that, Mr. Scary told us to form a line behind him. And then all three of us marched around and around the play-ground.

And guess what? My woodblock kept us in step very perfect!

After a while, we marched over to a microphone. It was on a stand in the grass.

"This is where you're going to sing, Sheldon," Mr. Scary said. "When you sing into this microphone, the whole audience will be able to hear you."

Mr. Scary smiled. "We won't turn it on yet. But you can still practice your song, okay?"

"Okay!" said Sheldon real thrilled.

Then he stood up straight and tall.

And he walked over to the microphone.

And he started to sing "Hark! Harold the Angel Sings."

He played the cymbals while he sang.

It was very lovely, sort of. But Mr. Scary's face did not look delighted.

He held up his hand. "Uh . . . could you hold it a second there, Sheldon?" he called. "Could you stop singing for a minute, please?"

Sheldon stopped.

Mr. Scary walked over to the microphone.

"Okay. Well . . . that's a *very* nice Christmas carol, Sheldon," he said. "And you were singing it beautifully. But the trouble is . . . it really isn't *Christmas,* is it?

So I'm wondering if maybe you know a different song."

Sheldon thought for a minute.

"How about 'I Have a Little Dreidel'?" he asked. "I know that one."

Mr. Scary ran his fingers through his tired hair.

"Yes, well, that's sort of the same problem, isn't it?" he said. "It's not really Hanukkah, either."

Mr. Scary bent down next to him.

"Do you know any songs besides holiday songs?" he asked. "Or is there some other talent you have, Sheldon? Like can you whistle, maybe? Or do a magic trick?"

Sheldon thought some more.

"I can blow milk bubbles out of my nose," he said. "But that mostly only happens when I'm choking."

Mr. Scary started rubbing the sides of his head. He was getting another headache in there, I think.

Then, all of a sudden, Sheldon's whole face lighted up.

"Hey! Wait! I just thought of another song I could sing!" he said. "'Happy Birthday,' Mr. Scary! I know all the words to 'Happy Birthday'! And that isn't even a holiday song!"

Our teacher stood there a second.

Then he nodded his head. And he said "Happy Birthday" would be just dandy.

Sheldon started his performance all over again.

He sang the song and played the cymbals very good.

After he got done, he did a somersault.

I do not know why.

Then hurray! Hurray! It was finally time for *me*!

I quick put down my woodblock. Then I reached into my pocket. And I took out my pretend lemons. And I started to pretend I was juggling.

Juggling for pretend is way easier than juggling for real.

I skipped and twirled and danced.

Mr. Scary and Sheldon clapped and clapped.

I did a bow.

Then I picked up my woodblock again. And I hit it with my stick. And me and Sheldon marched off the field.

We jumped all around and did a high five.

Then Sheldon picked me up and tried to twirl me around. Only he wasn't actually strong enough. And so mostly I just dragged on my toes.

His face turned reddish and sweaty.

He put me down and wiped his head with his sleeve.

"Whew. You weigh a ton, girl," he said.

I did a smile.

I like that odd boy.

I really, really do.

8

Halftime

                     Thursday

Dear first-grade journal,

  Yesterday when I got home from school Daddy was waiting for me.

  And ha! He had bought me a juggle book at the bookstore!

  It was for children six and up. And six and up is my EXACT age.

Daddy and I read each page very careful.

Then I did the whole entire book. Step by step.

And what do you know?

After I got done, I STILL COULDN'T JUGGLE!

I am getting fed up with this stupid talent.

Daddy said maybe I will learn it tomorrow.

That man is just kidding himself.

I am doomed.

       From,

       Junie B, First Grader

I closed my journal. And I watched the clock for the rest of the afternoon. 'Cause I just wanted to get home and practice some more.

Daddy came home from work to help me again. He tried to help me juggle for hours and hours and hours.

Only the most I could ever juggle was two dumb lemons.

And two dumb lemons is not even juggling.

Two dumb lemons is just throwing lemons in the air and catching them.

I am not going to school tomorrow.

And I *mean* it.

Friday

Dear first-grade journal,

I am at school.

    I do not know what went
wrong.
    On account of this morning I
told Mother I broke my leg.
    And then I limped and limped
all over the house.
    And the next thing you know,
I was on the bus.
    I am wearing the halftime
costume Mother made for me.
    My hat is made out of an
oatmeal box.
    I look like a nitwit.
        From,
        Junie B., First Grader

I glanced my eyes all around the room.

The children in Room One looked very cute.

The kickball players were wearing matching red-and-white shirts. All of their shirts said "*WE ARE (ROOM) NUMBER ONE!*"

The cheerleaders matched each other, too. They had on red skirts and white sweaters.

I looked at Sheldon.

His daddy's band jacket was way too giant. And his band hat came over his ears.

He looked like a nitwit, too.

I put my head down on my desk very glum.

My oatmeal-box hat fell on the floor.

May started to laugh.

"I hope that doesn't happen when you

juggle today, Junie Jones," she said very meanish.

She raised her eyebrows.

"You *are* going to juggle, *aren't* you?"

I didn't answer that girl.

Instead, I turned my head to the wall. And I closed my eyes. And I wished to turn invisible.

I wished and wished with all my might.

Then, finally, I opened my eyes again. And I turned back to May. And I stuck out my tongue at her.

She stuck out hers right back at me.

I did a sigh.

Bad news.

I wasn't invisible.

At ten o'clock we went to the softball field.

There were a million jillion parents there, I bet.

Mother and Daddy were sitting on the first row of the bleachers. Grampa and Grandma Miller were sitting right next to them. They were holding my baby brother named Ollie.

He was mooing.

All of them waved at me.

I did not wave back.

'Cause I was still trying to be invisible, of course.

Me and Sheldon sat down together.

He looked at the people in the bleachers. Then he quick turned around again. And he pulled his band hat over his face. And he giggled very nutty.

"Please stop doing that," I said. "You are just calling attention to ourself."

Sheldon put a cymbal on his head.

I rolled my eyes at that dumb guy. Then I hid my face in my skirt. And I didn't watch the tournament.

There were two games going on at once.

Room One was playing Room Two. And Room Three was playing Room Four.

I could hear the cheerleaders cheering real loud.

Room One was winning, I think.

I listened to the cheering for a very long time.

Then, all of a sudden, I heard lots of whistles and yelling.

I looked up to see what happened.

And oh no! Oh no!

Room One had just won the first game! And now it was time for *halftime*!

Mr. Scary came over to get us.

I tried to hide behind Sheldon. But Mr. Scary already saw me.

He said it is perfectly normal for me to be nervous. But I should just relax and try to enjoy myself.

"This is going to be a day you'll never forget," he told me.

My skin did a shiver. "Yeah, only that's exactly what I'm afraid of," I said.

After that, Mr. Scary took me and Sheldon by our hands. And he walked us to the field.

My legs felt like Silly String.

Mr. Scary went out to the microphone. And he made a 'nouncement to the people.

"Welcome to our halftime show, every-one," he said. "While Rooms One and Four are resting for the final game of the tournament, two of my students will present some very special entertainment."

He winked at me and Sheldon.

"Ladies and gentlemen . . . boys and girls . . . I am proud to present the musical genius of Sheldon Potts . . . and the unique talents of Junie B. Jones!"

As soon as he finished, he pointed at me and Sheldon. And he gave us the signal to go.

Sheldon did a whimper.

He did not move.

I looked at his face.

It was the color of paste.

Mr. Scary hurried over. And he gave Sheldon a nudge.

"Okay, you two. Go! Go! Go!" he said. "Take off!"

Very slow, I raised up my woodblock. And I hit it with my drumstick real light.

Tap.

"*Louder,*" said Mr. Scary. "You've got to play it louder, Junie B. And with a little bit of *pep*, okay?"

I took a big breath.

Tap . . . tap . . . tap.

Mr. Scary nodded. "Yes, yes! Better!" he said.

I swallowed hard.

TAP! TAP! TAP!

Mr. Scary gave me a thumbs-up. "That's *it*, Junie B.! That's *it*!" he said. "Keep it up!"

I kept it up.

TAP! TAP! TAP! TAP! TAP! TAP! TAP! TAP! TAP! TAP!

Then pretty soon, my feet started tapping, too! And they marched me right onto the field!

I looked behind me.

Sheldon was still standing on the sideline.

His face looked even pastier.

I ran back there and tugged on his arm.

"Come *on*, Sheldon! Let's go!" I said.

Sheldon plopped down in the grass.

"No, no! I can't, I can't!" he said.

I made a fist at that boy.

"Oh, yes, you *can*, Sheldon! You've *got* to! You've *got* to! This whole stupid show was your idea! And I'm NOT doing it by myself!"

After that, I helped Sheldon stand up. And I pulled him onto the field.

And *that's* when the worstest thing of all happened!

'Cause Room Two started laughing their heads off at us!

And it was the meanest laughing I ever
even *heard*!

Sheldon froze very stiff.

He stood there like a statue. And he
wouldn't even budge.

Then—all of a sudden—*CRASH!*

He dropped his cymbals.

And he ran across the playground as fast
as a speedboat!

One of the teachers ran after him. But Sheldon zoomed faster and faster.

Then he ran behind the swing sets.

And he circled around the monkey bars.

And he kept running and running till he was all the way behind the school.

And what do you know?

Sheldon never came back.

9

Plops

Room Two laughed even louder.

Rooms Three and Four laughed, too.

I *hated* that mean noise!

I hated it!

Tears came in my eyes. And my nose started sniffling very much.

I hanged my head so no one could see.

And ha!

That's when I spotted them!

Sheldon's cymbals!

They were still lying in the grass right next to my feet!

I quick picked them up. And I crashed them together so I wouldn't hear the laughing.

And it worked, I tell you! It worked! I couldn't hear the laughing at all!

That's how come I crashed them again . . . and again . . . and again, until my arms got tired.

And guess what?

When I finally stopped, no one was even laughing anymore.

I felt a little better.

Cymbals are very enjoyable.

After that, I stood in the middle of the field. And I rocked back and forth on my feet very thinking. 'Cause I didn't know what to do next, of course.

Just then, I heard shouting.

"BORRRRING!" yelled a voice.

"DON'T JUST STAND THERE . . . *DO* SOMETHING!" yelled a different voice.

I looked up. The boys who shouted were being taken away by their teacher.

But it was already too late.

More tears were coming in my eyes.

Mr. Scary started coming to get me.

My brain began to panic. 'Cause this was the stupidest halftime show I ever even saw.

The children started laughing again. They would be laughing at me for the rest of their life, probably!

Then, all of a sudden, my eyes glanced over to Sheldon's microphone.

And what do you know? A brand-*new* idea popped into my head!

And it's called, Hey! Maybe I could sing

a song just like Sheldon was going to do!

I grinned real big.

Yes! Yes!

I could sing "The Sun Will Come Out Tomorrow" from the hit musical *Annie*. 'Cause I love that tune, I tell you!

I hurried over to the microphone.

Then I opened my mouth to sing. Only I couldn't actually remember how that song started.

Mr. Scary was getting closer.

My brain panicked some more.

Then, out of nowhere, I heard a— *PLOP!*

I looked down.

Something had landed on the ground next to my boots.

I looked closer.

It was a flaky biscuit, I believe.

PLOP, PLOP, PLOP!

Two more biscuits. And a small plum.

Then suddenly, there was another fuss in the stands.

And two more kids were getting led away by their teacher.

That's when I got it.

That's when I figured out that those meanie kids had thrown *food* at me!

And throwing food is the biggest insult you can even do!

At first, my face turned red as a tomato.

Then I felt myself getting mad.

And I got madder . . .

And madder . . .

And then I picked up those biscuits!

And I started to throw them back!

Only all at once, my brain changed its mind!

And—instead of throwing them back— I put two of the biscuits in my *right* hand!

And I held the other biscuit in my *left* hand.

And then I tossed them in the air! One by one! *Exactly* like my juggle book said to.

And then, MAGIC HAPPENED, I TELL YOU!

It did! It *really* did!

Because for just a few teensy seconds, I juggled those biscuits way high in the air!

I juggled them as perfect as could be!

And I *caught* them, too!

I caught all *three* of those flaky guys.

And then the whole entire bleachers started to clap and clap and clap!

And then they cheered and cheered and cheered!

And the sound of that noise was better

than the bestest daydream I ever, ever had!

I did a bow.

The people kept on clapping.

I did another bow.

Then I picked up Sheldon's cymbals.

And I marched right off the field.

And guess what?

It was the proudest darned moment of my life.

The rest of the day was a joy.

We had a happy party. And I smiled till my cheeks hurt.

Also, I wrote in my journal again.

Friday afternoon

Dear first-grade journal,

We won the tournament!

Room One won the whole entire kickball tournament!

And so hurray, hurray! Mr.

Scary let us have a party for
the whole rest of the day!

   And guess what?

   They found Sheldon hiding
behind a bush. 'Cause he got
scared silly, ~~aparently~~ apparently. Only
finally he calmed himself down.
And now he is back to his
regular nutty self.

   And guess what else? I am
not even mad at him for
running away.

   On account of if Sheldon
didn't run away, I never would
have juggled, probably!

   Mother and Daddy hugged

me at the party. And Daddy
said I turned biscuits into
lemonade! And that is a hoot,
I tell you!
   And then Mother said the
bestest thing of all!
   She said, today I was a
STAR!!!
   And I really liked the sound
of that.
   Yup.
   I really, really did. ☺
         From,
      Junie B., First Grader

STAR

BARBARA PARK is one of today's funniest authors. Her Junie B. Jones books are consistently on the *New York Times* and *USA Today* bestseller lists. Her middle-grade novels, which include *Skinnybones, The Kid in the Red Jacket, Mick Harte Was Here,* and *The Graduation of Jake Moon,* have won over forty children's book awards. Barbara holds a B.S. in education. She has two grown sons and lives with her husband, Richard, in Arizona.

DENISE BRUNKUS'S entertaining illustrations have appeared in over fifty books. She lives in New Jersey with her husband and daughter.